W9-CKP-935

Disney

My Friends Tigger & Pooh

Calling All Piglets!

A Level 1 Early Reader

Copyright © 2010 Disney Enterprises, Inc.
All Rights Reserved. Based on the *Winnie the Pooh* works, by A.A. Milne and E.H. Shepard
Published by Dalmatian Press, LLC, in conjunction with Disney Enterprises, Inc.

Creative Edge, LLC, 2010. All rights reserved. Printed in the U.S.A.

The CREATIVE EDGE name is a trademark of Dalmatian Press, LLC, Franklin, Tennessee 37067. 1-800-815-8696
No part of this book may be reproduced or copied in any form without written permission from the copyright owner.

10 11 12 NGS 10 9 8 7 6 5 4 3 2 1
CE12417

One day, Piglet was
at his house.
It was a fall day.

"It is a good fall day," said Piglet.
"I like the wind.
I like the wind in the Wood.
I will go to the Wood."

Flap, flap, flap.

"What is that?" said Piglet.

Flap, flap, flap.

He looked and looked.
He saw something pink.
He saw something pink—flapping!

"It looks like me!" said Piglet.
"But I am Piglet.
   Two Piglets!
   How can that be?"

Piglet ran and ran!

He hid at a big rock.

Oh, no!

He saw something pink!

"Three Piglets!" said Piglet.

"How can that be?"

He ran and ran and ran!

He hid up a tall tree.

Oh, no!
He saw something pink!

"Four Piglets!" he said.
"How can that be?"

Piglet ran and ran.
"I will call
for help,"
he said.

SSuuuUUppppperrrr ssIIIEEEUUtthhs!

Piglet called the Super Sleuths,
Pooh, Darby, Tigger, and Buster.
"Time to slap my cap!" said Darby.

The Super Sleuths saw the flag.
The flag had Piglet's house.
"We will help you, Piglet!" called Pooh.

"Any time, any place,
The Super Sleuths are on the case!"

"I saw three Piglets!" said Piglet.
"Three Piglets in pink!"

"Think, think, think,"
said Darby.
"Three Piglets in pink.
How can that be?"

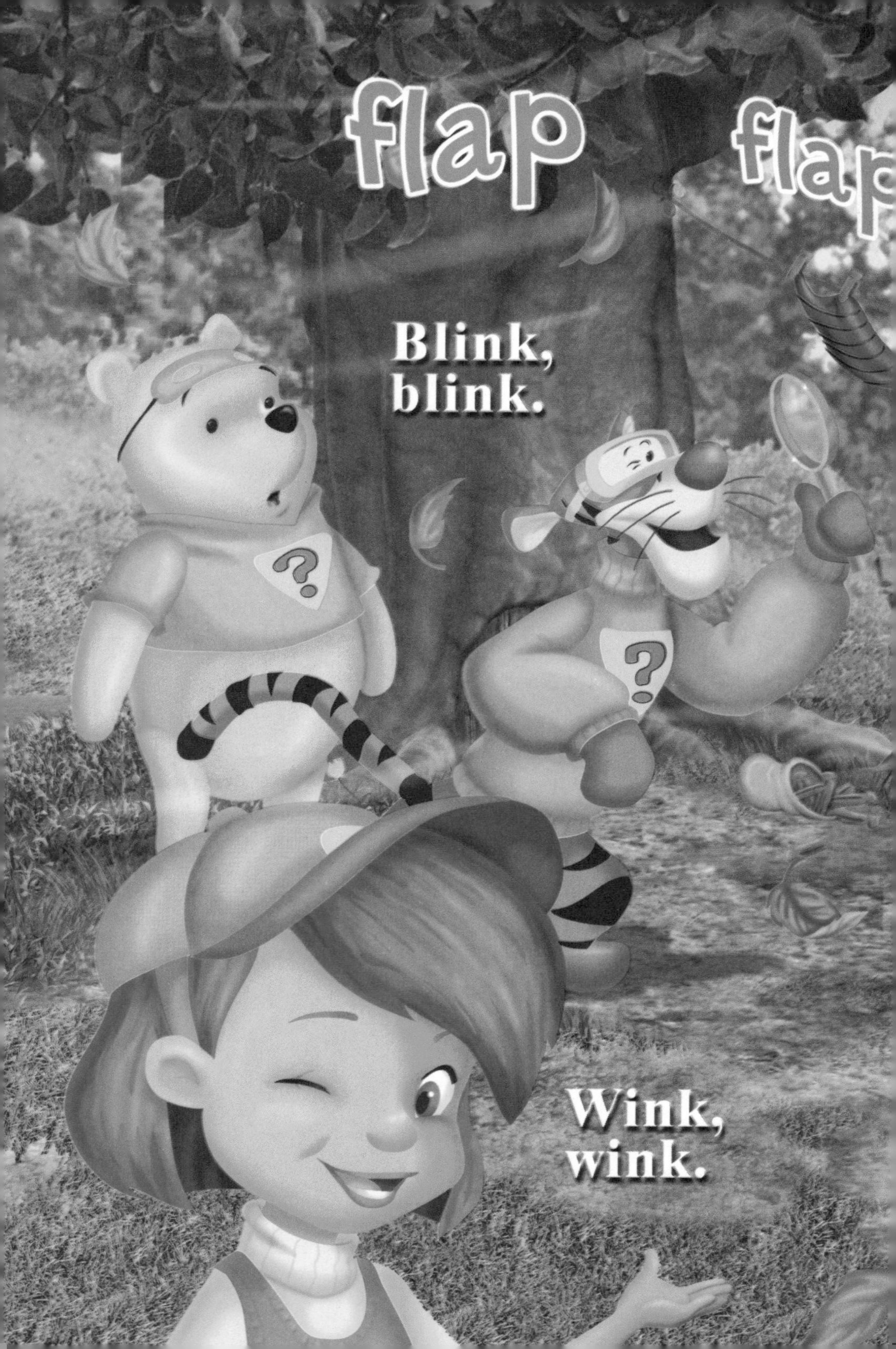

Blink,
blink.

Wink,
wink.

"I see a lot of pink, too," Darby said.
"Think, Piglet. Where did you see
  the pink?"
"In the Wood," said Piglet. "Come on!"

Piglet took all the
Super Sleuths to the Wood.
"Calling all Piglets!"
called Darby.

"Aha! Yes!" said Tigger.
"I see something pink!"

"Hmmm…" said Pooh.
"I see something pink!"

"Look!" said Darby.
"I see something pink!"

"Oh, my," said Piglet.
"Three pink tops. The tops are
off the three Piglets!"

Darby hugged Piglet.
"No," she said. "All the tops are
your tops. At your house,
the big wind shook your tops..."

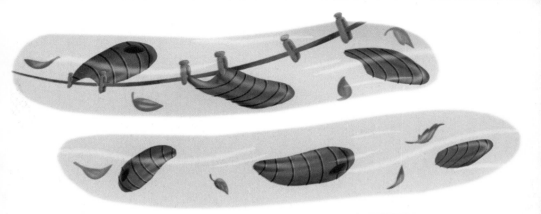

"And took
your tops,"
said Tigger.

"And, look!
Your tops are
in the Wood!"
said Pooh.

"Oh," said Piglet.
"It was the big wind.
It was not three Piglets."

"I like one Piglet.

One Piglet is good," said Pooh.

"Thank you, Pooh," said Piglet.